the Milo & Jazz MYSTE

3

THE CASE OF THE
Haunted HAUNTEd HOUSE

by Lewis B. Montgomery
illustrated by Amy Wummer

The KANE PRESS
New York

Text copyright © 2009 by Lewis B. Montgomery
Illustrations copyright © 2009 by Amy Wummer
Super Sleuthing Strategies illustrations copyright © 2009 by Kane Press, Inc.
Super Sleuthing Strategies illustrations by Nadia DiMattia

Library of Congress Cataloging-in-Publication Data

Montgomery, Lewis B.
The case of the haunted haunted house / by Lewis B. Montgomery ;
illustrated by Amy Wummer.
p. cm. — (The Milo & Jazz mysteries ; 3)
Summary: Amateur detectives Milo and Jazz try to figure out if the haunted
house they are building for the school fair has a real ghost.
ISBN 978-1-57565-295-5 (pbk.) — ISBN 978-1-57565-297-9 (library binding)
[1. Haunted houses—Fiction. 2. Schools—Fiction. 3. Mystery and detective
stories.] I. Wummer, Amy, ill. II. Title.
PZ7.M7682Cah 2009
[Fic]—dc22
2008049804

10 9 8 7 6 5 4 3 2 1

First published in the United States of America in 2009 by Kane Press, Inc.
Printed in Hong Kong

Book Design: Edward Miller

The Milo & Jazz Mysteries is a registered trademark of Kane Press, Inc.

www.kanepress.com

For Wilton, Rose, Harrison, and Abbey

—L.B.M.

CHAPTER ONE

"Chicken fingers." Milo pulled one off his lunch tray and looked at it. "If these are the fingers, how big is the chicken?"

His friend Jazz laughed. "Big enough to eat *us* for lunch."

A hand reached over Jazz's shoulder and grabbed her oatmeal cookie. She twisted around. "Hey! Give that back!"

Grinning down at them, Jazz's older brother Chris took a huge bite. "Better get used to it." He handed her what was left of the cookie and headed back across the cafeteria toward his buddies.

"You haven't won yet!" Jazz yelled after him.

"What was *that* about?" Milo asked.

She sighed. "I bet him my desserts for a whole week that our booth for Spring Thing would raise more money than his."

Milo stared at her. "But his class is going to run Dunk the Teacher. That booth always does the best."

Jazz looked stubborn. "We'll just have to think of something better."

Milo thought about it as they ate their lunch. What could they come up with to beat Dunk the Teacher? "How about a petting zoo?" he said. "Everybody with a pet could bring it in. You could bring Bitsy." Bitsy was Jazz's potbellied pig.

Jazz's face brightened. Then she frowned. "Ms. Ali won't let us. Not since Gordy hid his hamster in her desk and it pooped on a pop quiz. Remember? She said no more pets the whole rest of the year."

"Oh, yeah," Milo said.

As they walked back to class, he had another idea. "I know! A Sleuth Booth. *We solve mysteries on the spot.*"

Milo and Jazz were detectives in training. They got lessons in the mail from world-famous private eye Dash Marlowe. With a little help from Dash, they solved real-life mysteries.

Jazz shook her head. "What if we can't solve a mystery on the spot? Besides, it's supposed to be the whole class, not just you and me."

Good point, Milo thought. That was Jazz. Always thinking logically. It used to drive him nuts. But now he had to admit, she really was a great partner.

Back in class, Ms. Ali clapped her hands twice. "Okay, everybody, settle down. It's time to come up with a booth idea for the Spring Thing—"

Brooke Whitley's hand shot up.

On the blackboard: History test on Friday! Early dismissal days: Tuesdays

"Yes, Brooke?"

"I think we should do a makeover booth." She tossed her long hair and smiled smugly at her friends, Emily S. and Emily B. The Emilies smiled back.

The boys in the back of the room made gagging noises. Gordy yelled, "Makeup? No way!"

Brooke glared at him.

"Gordy, that's enough." Ms. Ali
looked around. "Any other ideas?"

"Bean bag toss?" Randy said.

Someone groaned.

"Balloon animals!" Spencer called out.

"Do you know how to make them?"
Ms. Ali asked.

He frowned. "Well . . . I could maybe
do a snake."

Emily B. raised her hand.

"Yes, Emily?"

"Brooke's idea is the best, and *I* think we should vote for it right now." She beamed at Brooke.

Milo shot a glance at Jazz. She was staring out the window, chin in hand. Probably thinking of the week of desserts she'd kissed goodbye.

Ms. Ali sighed. "All right. All in favor of a makeover booth—"

Jazz sat up suddenly.

"Wait!" she called out. "How about a haunted house?"

CHAPTER TWO

An excited buzz ran through the classroom.

"Haunted houses are for Halloween," Brooke said.

"Playland Park has one year round," said Frida. "It's my favorite ride."

"Mine, too!" someone else called out.

Brooke scowled at Jazz. "Spring Thing is held outdoors, remember? How are we supposed to build a haunted house?"

Jazz smiled. "We don't have to." She pointed out the open window. "We can use the learning cottage."

The learning cottage was a trailer that had been used as a classroom while repairs were being done on the school. Ever since, the trailer had stood empty.

Emily B. raised her hand again. "*I* think a haunted house would be too scary for the little kids."

"Not as scary as a first grader in make-up," Gordy muttered.

Everybody laughed.

"That's a good point, Emily," Ms. Ali said. "It needs to be for the whole school, not just the upper grades."

Milo said, "My little brother Ethan loves the haunted house at Playland Park." On their last trip, Ethan had gone through the haunted house almost as many times as the Dino Safari.

Ms. Ali still looked doubtful, but she called for a vote.

Everybody voted for the haunted house—except Brooke and the Emilies.

Emily S. started to lift her hand, but Brooke and Emily B. glared at her and she yanked it down. Her feet tapped nervously under her desk.

"All right," Ms. Ali said. "Haunted house it is. But please, let's not go overboard. We don't want any crying kindergartners."

Gordy called out, "Does that mean no making them eat fake eyeballs and brains and stuff?"

Ms. Ali shook her head and sighed. "Time to get out your math books."

All the kids groaned, including Milo. Then he had an idea. They were working on measurements—

"Ms. Ali, couldn't we go measure the learning cottage?" he asked. "To see how

16

much spooky stuff will fit? You're always saying we should use math in real life."

Ms. Ali thought for a second. Then she smiled. "Why not?"

The class cheered.

When they reached the learning cottage, Milo saw that the door hung slightly open and the lock was broken.

"I'll let Mr. Schiff know," Ms. Ali said. Mr. Schiff was the school custodian.

Inside, the floor was a sea of broken chalk and crumpled papers. A desk with a missing leg lay on its side in the middle of the room. Someone had piled chairs in one corner. In another, rolled-up posters gathered dust.

Gordy let out a long whistle. "What a mess!"

"At least we know nobody else is using the place," Jazz said.

Ms. Ali nodded. "I'll ask Mr. Schiff if he can clear this out."

Milo looked around. Those big sheets of cardboard would be great for tombstones, he thought. They were a little old and ratty, but who wants a clean new tombstone in a haunted house? And that globe was falling off its stand. Maybe they could wrap it in black plastic and use it for the body of a giant spider.

He told his classmates what he was thinking.

Jazz said, "I'll bet there's all kinds of stuff in here that we could use. Hey, maybe we can clean the place up ourselves!"

Brooke wrinkled her nose. "Who wants to *clean*?"

"Not me," Emily B. said quickly. She wrinkled her nose like Brooke. Milo thought she looked like a beady-eyed squirrel.

"I think it's a great idea," Ms. Ali said. "If we offer to clean up, the principal might be more likely to approve our plan."

As Milo pulled out the measuring tape, he caught a glimpse of Brooke staring at Jazz, eyes narrowed. If Emily B. looked like a squirrel, Brooke reminded him of something else.

An angry snake about to strike.

CHAPTER THREE

Later in the afternoon, when they got back from gym, Ms. Ali had a big smile on her face. "I asked the principal if we could use the learning cottage for our haunted house—and he said yes."

"Can we stay after school and clean?" Jazz asked.

Brooke tossed her hair. "Emily S.'s grandma is picking us up today. We're going skating, just the two of us."

She smiled as Emily B. shot Emily S. a jealous look. Ducking her head, Emily S. opened her desk and began shuffling papers and books around.

Ms. Ali asked who wanted to stay and clean. Jazz and Milo raised their hands, along with a few others.

When the bell rang, the volunteers loaded up on cleaning supplies and headed for the empty trailer. But halfway there, Milo realized he'd left his spelling homework behind. He dropped his mop and bucket and ran back.

Emily S. knelt on the floor next to a pile of stuff spilling out of her backpack.

Brooke stood over her. "Come on. What could be so major? We're going to miss open-skate time at the rink." She sniffed. "Maybe I should have done something with Emily B. instead."

Milo picked up some stray papers and handed them over to Emily S. Pink-faced, she stuffed them in her backpack and followed Brooke out.

Yikes, Milo thought. Even Brooke's

friends were scared of her. He found his spelling sheet and stuffed it in his pocket.

When he got back to the learning cottage, Jazz called him over. "The big black bag by Carlos is for trash. Spencer's got the recycling box. And this—" She lifted a white plastic bag. "This is the lost and found. It's for whatever we're not sure we should throw out."

"How about the things we want to keep for the haunted house?" Milo asked.

She pointed. "In that corner."

He went over to take a look. Wow, what a pile! He pulled out a poster and unrolled it. A pair of kittens reading *The Cat in the Hat*? For a haunted house? And how in the world were they going to use a jigsaw puzzle of the rainforest?

Haunted houses needed *scary* stuff.
Skeletons. Axes dripping with fake
blood. Pictures with eyes that followed
you around and creepy things like—

Suddenly a hand shot out and
clamped around his ankle.

Milo screamed.

CHAPTER FOUR

The pile fell over, and Gordy climbed out laughing. "Oh, man. That was great. You should have seen your face."

Milo stomped away. Shoving the puzzle in the lost-and-found bag, he grumbled, "Gordy and his stupid jokes."

Jazz nodded sympathetically as she tossed in a DVD. "Tell me about it. Remember the time he tried to tie my sneaker to my chair?"

For the next half hour everyone worked steadily, even Gordy. Carlos found some yellow streamers they could use to make a mummy. Spencer swept the floor, and Jazz and Pria carried out the trash. Milo took the lost-and-found bag to the front office, but the door was locked, so he dropped it in the back of their classroom closet.

"This is going to be the best Spring Thing booth ever," he told Jazz as they walked home together. "Wait till Chris hears. He'll be sorry he ever made that bet."

"I hope he doesn't hear too soon," Jazz said. "Chris hates to lose."

Milo shrugged. It wasn't as if her brother could do anything about it. How could Dunk the Teacher compete with a haunted house?

The next morning when Milo got to school, he saw a crowd of kids staring and pointing at the learning cottage.

"What's going on?" he asked a kindergartner.

She looked up at him with wide eyes. "They say it's haunted."

Milo laughed. "It isn't really haunted. We're just making it into a haunted house for the Spring Thing."

The girl looked doubtful. "Are you sure?"

"Sure I'm sure." He spotted Jazz and pointed. "It was her idea."

Jazz walked up to them. "Some kid just told me there's a ghost inside the learning cottage."

A third grader turned around. "I heard that it groans and rattles chains." He let out a long, eerie groan.

The kindergartner burst into tears.

Jazz took her hand. "Don't cry. There isn't any ghost. Come on. I'll take you in and show you."

"No!" The girl snatched her hand away and ran off.

"This is ridiculous," Jazz fumed.

Milo shrugged. "I don't know. It could be good. Like advertising for our haunted house, right?"

"Not if kids are scared to go inside," she pointed out.

"That's just one kindergartner being a baby," Milo said.

Jazz still looked worried. "What if Ms. Ali hears what they're saying? Maybe she'll decide a haunted house is too scary for little kids after all. Maybe she'll shut us down."

Oh.

All that cleaning. All that planning. He would hate to see it wasted, that was for sure. Then he thought of something he'd hate even more: helping to run a makeover booth.

The school bell rang, and kids lined up to go inside.

"You're right," he told Jazz. "We'd better do something about this crazy rumor—and quick!"

CHAPTER FIVE

At recess, Milo waited for Jazz at the flagpole. "I think we should find out how this rumor started."

Jazz shrugged. "Probably a kid said something about our haunted house, and some other kid heard it wrong."

"I guess," Milo said. But their whole class knew all about the plans for the Spring Thing. Wouldn't somebody have set it straight?

They split up. Milo headed to the playground, where a gaggle of first-grade girls were clustered on the jungle gym. When he mentioned the learning cottage, they shrieked.

"I heard the ghost was a boy who died a long, long time ago," one girl said. "His mean teacher locked him in the closet and forgot about him."

"They only put that trailer in last year," Milo told her. "I think we would have heard if someone died in it."

The girl looked disappointed. "Well, maybe he died somewhere else and then moved to the learning cottage because it was nicer."

Right, Milo thought. "Listen, I just want to know who told you it was haunted."

They all looked at one another.

"I heard it from her—"

"Well, *she* told *me,* and *I* told—"

"No, you didn't! We heard it at the same time, then *you*—"

Milo gave up and walked away.

A group of bigger kids was gathered on the basketball court. He spotted Jazz at the edge of the crowd.

When he came up, she said, "I think I found our rumor starter." She nodded at a tall boy at the center of the circle. "Cody claims he saw a ghost last night inside the learning cottage."

"What was he doing here at night?" Milo asked.

"He lives right over there, in that blue house across from Emily S." Jazz pointed. "I know because he's on my brother Chris's football team."

Cody was telling the kids about the

ghostly light he had seen bobbing around in the learning cottage.

"And that's not all," Cody went on. "I *heard* it, too. It went like this." He let out a long, low moan. A few of the girls screamed and giggled. Cody smirked.

"What did you find inside?" Jazz asked.

Cody looked startled. "Inside what?"

"What do you think?" Jazz said. "The learning cottage. Didn't you go in?"

Everybody looked at Cody.

Quickly he said, "Sure. I mean, I tried. But it was like there was this force field all around. I just kept hitting it and bouncing off. Crazy!"

"Crazy is right," Jazz grumbled as the bell rang and they all lined up. "I think Cody was too scared to go inside, so he made up that stupid force-field story."

She probably was right, Milo thought. Still, that didn't mean Cody had made up the whole thing. If he'd been scared, something had scared him. A bobbing light. Moaning.

A crawly feeling crept up Milo's back. What if there really *was* a ghost?

CHAPTER SIX

To Milo and Jazz's relief, Ms. Ali didn't seem to have heard the ghost rumors. Teachers were strange. They always knew if you had gum in your mouth and when they should call on you because you didn't know the answer. But they never seemed to notice the important stuff.

It was art day, and the art teacher let

them work on their haunted house. They broke up into groups. Milo, Jazz, and Frida made a cardboard coffin lid that would fly open when anyone walked by. Other kids took on the tombstones and the giant spider.

Gordy's group was the most popular.

He organized half of them to build a
guillotine. The other half worked on a
dummy with a head that flew off when
the blade came down. To Gordy's
dismay, the art teacher drew the line at
fake blood spattering all over people who
came through the haunted house.

Brooke refused to help, and went off to a desk to draw fashion designs. Emily B. tossed her ponytail and followed.

Emily S. stood watching Jazz and Milo, tapping her foot nervously. Just as she took a step toward them, Brooke hissed at her from the corner. Throwing the coffin one last glance, Emily S. turned to join her friends.

Jazz had karate after school, so Milo walked home alone. Waiting for him in the mailbox was an envelope. It said DM in the upper left-hand corner.

A lesson from Dash!

DASH MARLOWE
SECRETS OF A SUPER SLEUTH!

Cause and Effect

Why did the suspect cross the road?

(a) Why not?

(b) Who cares?

(c) To get to the other side, obviously.

If you answered (a) or (b), you are not thinking like a detective. To solve a case, you often need to look at **motive**—why people do the things they do. The motive is the cause. The crime is the effect. One leads to the other.

And if you answered (c)? Sorry—you're still not thinking like a detective. Sure, people usually cross the road to get to the other side. But remember, the most obvious motive is not always the real one!

Once, in my early detecting days, I was called in to investigate strange noises coming from a sea cave at night. Local fishermen refused to go near the place. Shaking with fear, one of them whispered that the sounds were from an ancient monster rising from the bottom of the ocean.

Of course, world-famous private eye Dash Marlowe does not believe in sea monsters. So I asked myself, "What could cause someone to sneak into a dark, damp, chilly cave?"

I was sure I knew the answer. It must be the gang of smugglers I'd been tailing. I planned to capture them single-handedly, find their hidden loot, and win a huge reward.

At low tide, I went down to the cave. Cautiously, I crept inside. The darkness grew deeper and deeper, to pitch black.

My flashlight flickered feebly.

Suddenly I heard a noise. I sprang!

A thump, another thump, a groan—and I had my prisoner. I shone the light into his face.

But it wasn't a smuggler. It was the fearful fisherman! He admitted that he had invented the "sea monster." But what in the world was his motive?

When I questioned him, he told me he had done it to get out of fishing. He was tired of tuna. He was sick of salmon. And he'd had it up to here with halibut. What he really wanted was to get his village on the TV news. He hoped that would attract crowds of tourists, and then he could open up a fancy hotel.

We were lying in a puddle, so I let him go. As I slogged home, wet and shivering, I swore that next time I would think a little harder about motive.

Motive, Milo thought. Who would
have a reason to be in the empty learning
cottage after dark? Not the custodian.
Mr. Schiff hated it when after-school
activities ran late. He said his cat got
grumpy if he wasn't home by five.

Could someone be using the learning
cottage for a criminal purpose? But
what?

Milo turned back to Dash's lesson.

To find the motive, you need to think like your suspects. Put yourself in their shoes. (I nearly broke my neck doing this in The Case of the Roller-Skating Robber, but that's another story. . . .)

So, why did the suspect cross the road? If you want to be a world-famous private eye like me, Dash Marlowe, the answer is (d): I don't know yet, but I'm going to find out!

The lesson went on, with tips on how to get the truth from suspects. Dash said if you watched their body language, you could tell if they were nervous—which might mean they were hiding something.

There were lots of signs: looking away, fidgeting, arm-crossing, blinking, touching the mouth while talking, swallowing a lot. . . .

As soon as he finished his homework, Milo headed over to Jazz's house.

After she read the lesson, he said, "I can't think of any reason why someone would be in the learning cottage. Can you?"

Jazz shrugged. "Maybe Cody made the whole thing up."

"Why would he do that?" Milo asked.

"To get attention?" Jazz said.

"Or maybe—" Milo gulped. "Maybe there *is* a ghost."

"Milo, be serious—" She broke off. "Hang on. That could be it."

"You think the place is haunted?" *Yikes.* If even *Jazz* believed . . .

"Of course not!" she said. "But what if that's the motive?"

"I don't get it," Milo said.

Jazz bounced on her toes. "What if someone *wants* the kids at school to think it's haunted? What if someone sneaked in at night dressed as a ghost? Fluttered around. Flashed a light."

"But why?"

"A joke?" she said.

They looked at each other. Then Milo said what they were both thinking.

"Gordy!"

CHAPTER SEVEN

Of course! They should have thought of Gordy right away. It was just the kind of thing that he would do.

Jazz frowned. "But Gordy loves the haunted house. He wouldn't want Ms. Ali to shut it down."

"Maybe he didn't think of that," Milo said. When it came to jokes, Gordy never seemed to think. Period.

Still, everyone in the class knew that if Ms. Ali decided their haunted house was too scary, she might shut it down. And nobody would want that to—

Suddenly a picture flashed into Milo's mind: an angry snake about to strike.

"Brooke!" he said. "She was mad about your idea getting chosen over hers. Maybe she wanted to get even."

Flipping open her little purple notebook, Jazz wrote:

Suspect	Motive
Brooke	Revenge—mad that her idea wasn't chosen
Gordy	Loves to play jokes and scare people

Jazz tapped her pen against her teeth and frowned. "There's someone else who wouldn't want our haunted house to do well."

"Who?" he asked.

"Chris."

Milo had almost forgotten about the bet. "But he's your brother. Would he really sink that low?"

"I hope not. But he *hates* to lose a bet. One time he rolled in poison ivy just to win a bet with his best friend about who'd get it worse."

"Gross," said Milo.

Jazz went back to her list and added: *Chris—wants to win the bet.*

Milo thought about what Dash had said. *Think like your suspects. Put yourself in their shoes.*

But which shoes? Chris's football cleats? Gordy's untied sneakers? Or Brooke's super-stylish boots?

All three suspects had strong motives. Any one of them could be the ghost.

Or the ghost could be . . . a ghost.

He quickly pushed that thought aside. Okay. What would Dash do?

"Question the suspects," Milo said aloud.

Jazz nodded. "Let's talk to Chris."

They found him by the front door, getting ready to go out.

"Chris, wait," Jazz said. "We want to ask you something. It's about the bet."

Her brother grinned. "Don't waste your breath. That bet was fair and square. You're not weaseling out now."

Milo stared at Chris. Did he look nervous? Was he hiding anything?

Jazz put her hands on her hips. "I'm not weaseling. Haven't you heard about our haunted house?"

"So what? You haven't got a chance. Those desserts are mine. *Mmm. . . .*"

Rubbing his stomach, Chris left.

Jazz was fuming. "What does he mean, we haven't got a chance?"

"Maybe he means he's going to make sure we lose," Milo said. "Maybe he really is the one haunting the learning cottage. Where's he going, anyway?"

They looked at each other. Then they ran to the door.

It was getting dark, but they could see by the glow of the streetlights. Chris was starting down the block already, walking fast. They hurried after him.

Chris turned the corner.

Milo whispered, "Look! He's heading toward the school!"

They followed, keeping as far behind as they could without losing sight of

her brother. Chris glanced back once, but didn't seem to see them.

As they drew closer to the school, Milo's mind was a whirl. Had they solved the case? Was Chris the ghost?

But Chris walked right past the school. He went up to a house and rang the bell. The door opened, and he went in.

So much for that.

Milo sighed. "Oh, well. Let's go."

Jazz didn't move. She was staring at the house. "Milo, that's Cody's house."

"Yeah, so? You said they're on a football team together, right?"

"Exactly!" Jazz said. "Don't you see? Chris wanted to get our haunted house shut down. But he knew I'd find out if he spread the ghost rumors himself.

So Chris got Cody to pretend he saw a ghost."

"You mean . . . Cody didn't really see a spooky light?" Milo said slowly.

"Of course not. Aren't you listening? They made it up."

Milo pointed at the learning cottage. "Then what's *that?*"

CHAPTER EIGHT

Milo and Jazz stared at the light bobbing in the window of the learning cottage.

"This is great!" Jazz said.

Milo's stomach fluttered. "It is?"

"Let's go!" She dashed off, then turned back. "Are you coming, or what?"

"Um . . . what?" he mumbled.

Hands on hips, Jazz stared at him. "Don't you want to catch the ghost?"

Slowly he followed her. Sure, they wanted to catch the ghost. But what if the ghost caught them first?

They headed toward the flickering light, Jazz in the lead. Almost there—

OOMPH!

Something heavy slammed into Milo, knocking him down and pinning him to the ground. A bright light shone straight into his face.

"Gotcha!" a boy's voice said.

"Chris?" said Jazz.

The light swung away, and the weight lifted off Milo. He pushed up to his feet.

"See, I told you, Cody," Chris said. "There's no ghost. It's just my sister faking ghost stuff to get kids all stoked about her lame-o haunted house."

"ME?" Jazz yelled. "You're the one trying to get us shut down so you can win the bet!"

As they both started shouting at once, Milo looked toward the learning cottage. The light was gone.

Milo shivered. Was it a real ghost, or just a person? Either way, their noise seemed to have scared it off. Milo wasn't sure if he was disappointed or relieved.

Jazz and Chris argued the whole way home. Chris said he'd caught them red-handed, and threatened to tell the principal. Jazz said *they* had caught *him* red-handed, and threatened to tell their parents.

"When we saw the light inside the learning cottage, we were all outside," Milo pointed out. "How could any of us be the ghost?"

Chris didn't look convinced. "Maybe you got a friend to go in there."

Jazz crossed her arms. "Or *you* did."

This wasn't getting them anywhere.

Milo wondered how Dash Marlowe would deal with a pair of squabbling siblings.

"What about our other suspects?" he asked Jazz.

Her eyes widened. "Brooke and Gordy! We haven't even questioned them yet."

Chris agreed to call a truce—for now. But he said they'd better find the real ghost soon. If they couldn't . . .

"Then your haunted house is history." Chris smirked.

The next morning, they went straight to work. They found Brooke on the swings, flanked by the Emilies.

"We want to talk to you," Jazz said.

"Oh, yeah?" Brooke crossed her arms.

Milo tried to remember what Dash had said about crossed arms. Wasn't that one of the signs that a suspect was nervous?

"Have you heard about the learning cottage ghost?" Jazz asked.

"Sure. All the kids are talking about it." Brooke swallowed. Another sign!

Jazz went on. "We don't believe it's a real ghost. We think someone has been sneaking in there after dark."

Brooke swallowed again. *Wow*, Milo thought. She must be nervous, all right—though he never would have guessed it from the snooty look on her face.

Emily S. seemed nervous, too, the way she was tapping her feet in the dirt. But then again, she always did that.

Jazz stared Brooke straight in the eyes. "Well? Was it you? Are you the learning cottage ghost?"

Brooke's fingers moved to her mouth. Another sign!

The fingers came out holding a big chewed-up wad of gum. Daintily, Brooke placed it in a foil wrapper.

Gum! Milo gave himself a mental

smack in the head. No wonder she kept swallowing.

Brooke said, "Why in the world would I pretend to be a ghost?"

"You didn't want the haunted house," Milo said. "Maybe you're trying to ruin it. If Ms. Ali finds out that all the little kids are scared—*Ow!*" He stared at Jazz, who had just jabbed him in the ribs.

Brooke smiled. It wasn't a nice smile. "If Ms. Ali finds out, then goodbye, haunted house. Right?" She laughed. "Better hope nobody tells her."

Brooke marched off, with the Emilies trailing behind her.

Jazz glared at Milo. "I can't believe you said that! Now Brooke's going to run straight to Ms. Ali."

"If she's the haunter, she already thought of it," Milo said.

"And if she isn't?"

Jazz was so annoyed, she insisted on questioning Gordy alone. "You can go and look for clues at the scene of the crime."

Milo stared at the learning cottage. "You want me to go in there? By myself?"

Jazz raised an eyebrow. "Don't tell me you really think it's haunted."

Crossing his arms, he looked away and swallowed. "Of course not."

Slowly he crossed the parking lot. Anyway, it was daytime, he told himself. And with all these people around, nothing could happen to him. Right?

Milo pushed the door open.

It was dark and gloomy inside. He flipped the switch, and mysterious shapes appeared in the dim light.

With Gordy in charge, the class had put in blue and green light bulbs and thrown sheets over the desks and chairs. Fake cobwebs hung in the corners.

Gordy was really good at this haunting thing. Maybe he *was* the culprit.

Milo edged his way into the room. It was pretty spooky, even in the daytime.

Don't be a chicken, he told himself. *Pretend you're Dash Marlowe in the deep, dark cave. Shining your flashlight all around. Searching for smugglers and hidden treasure . . .*

Wait a minute.

Searching . . .

Searching with a flashlight . . . for something hidden in the dark.

That was it!

CHAPTER Nine

On the playground, Jazz shook her head. "The ghost isn't the sea monster, it's Dash? Milo, you're not making any sense."

He tried to explain more clearly. "What if we got the motive wrong? Maybe whoever was in the learning cottage wasn't trying to scare anyone. Maybe they were looking for something.

That's why they'd need a light—to search in the dark!"

"What could they be looking for? There's nothing in there but a bunch of haunted-house stuff."

"There *used* to be more. Remember all that junk we cleaned out? What if we got rid of something someone wanted?"

Jazz frowned. "Anything that wasn't trash, we took to the lost and found."

Hmm. She was right.

Wait . . .

"That bag never got to the lost and found!" Milo said. "The office was locked, so I stuck it in our classroom closet, and, well—I guess I forgot about it."

They stared at each other. Then they bolted toward the school.

"Bathroom!" Jazz gasped as they squeezed past the startled recess monitor. They raced down the hall.

The bag was still in the back of the closet, right where Milo had left it. They dumped it out on the floor.

Milo scanned the mess. Which item could be important enough to make somebody sneak into the learning cottage after dark—twice?

Not the kitty poster, that was for sure. Not the jigsaw puzzle, even if it wasn't missing pieces. Definitely not a sheet of dopey stickers saying Super-Duper Reader!

He picked up a spiral notebook and leafed through it, but all it had in it were math problems. Unless they were a secret code . . .

Then Jazz held up a DVD in a blank case. "What's this?"

They ran over to the classroom computer.

Jazz slid in the DVD and they waited,

breathless, until a video started playing onscreen.

A girl stood on a stage. As the camera moved in, Milo saw that she wore a pink fuzzy romper, like a baby. On her head was a pink bonnet, and over the romper . . .

"Oh, no. Please tell me that's not a *bib*!" Jazz said.

Music started: *"Baby face. You've got the cutest little baby face. . . ."*

The girl began to tap dance.

Who was she? If only the camera would zoom in a little closer.

Wrapped up in watching, Milo and Jazz didn't notice footsteps coming up behind them.

The song was just ending. With a final

tap and twirl, the girl stopped and the
camera zoomed in on her face.

"*Emily!*" said a voice behind them.

Milo and Jazz spun around. Brooke
and the Emilies stood in the doorway,
staring at the screen.

Milo looked at Emily S. "It was you, wasn't it? You were the one who sneaked into the learning cottage. You were searching for this DVD you dropped."

Emily didn't answer.

"The light in the window—that was your flashlight. And the moaning . . ." He frowned. "Well, I guess you must have been upset when you couldn't find what you were looking for."

Emily S. burst into tears. "I tried so hard to find that DVD before anyone else did! I knew if it got out, the whole school would make fun of me."

Milo glanced at Jazz.

Did Dash feel sorry for the people he caught?

Then Brooke said, "Oh, Emily, stop crying. *Nobody* in this school is going to make fun of any friend of mine. Besides, I happen to think tap dancing is totally cool."

Sniffling, Emily S. stared at her. "You do?"

"Sure," Brooke said. "And you're really good! But the baby thing . . ."

Emily S. smiled through her tears. "My mom made me dress up that way. Yuck."

She turned to Milo and Jazz. "Are you going to tell?"

The two detectives looked at each other. Then Jazz popped the DVD out of the computer and handed it to Emily S.

"Of course not," Jazz said. "It's over, right? No more haunting in the haunted house."

Emily S. wiped her eyes and took the DVD. Then, to Milo's surprise, Brooke smiled at Jazz. A real smile—not even a snaky one!

Of course, as soon as Brooke smiled, Emily B. smiled too.

She still looked like a squirrel.

ENTER AT YOUR OWN RISK!

CHAPTER TEN

Milo pushed aside the tattered gauze and peered out through the window of the learning cottage.

"Check out that crowd!" he said to Jazz. "Our haunted house is definitely the most popular booth at the fair. Chris hasn't got a chance."

"Actually, we agreed to drop the bet."

"You did? Why?"

"Mom is on one of her health kicks." Jazz sighed. "When dessert is spinach smoothies, who wants seconds?"

Too bad about the bet, Milo thought. But at least they had solved their case! He couldn't wait to report to Dash.

Bang! Behind him, the coffin lid flew open. A zombie sat up and looked at Jazz.

"Will you get away from that window!" it ordered in Gordy's voice. "You're supposed to be kneeling behind the coffin so you can tap on it when someone walks by. Otherwise I won't know when to pop out."

"Okay, okay! Keep your rotting pants on." Jazz tucked in a loose end of her mummy costume and took her place.

A skeleton asked Milo, "Do I look okay?"

"You look kind of bony to me." He laughed. "Get it? Bony?"

The skeleton tapped her foot. "I'm nervous. What if I mess up?"

"Are you kidding? Your tap-dancing skeleton act is the best part of the whole haunted house. I'm so glad we found out about your hidden talent!"

Under her skull mask, Emily S. made a face. "I still can't believe I dropped that awful DVD. My mom made me bring it to school that day so I could give it to my grandma when she picked me up."

"The baby costume *was* pretty bad," Milo said. "But your tap dancing isn't awful. It's awe*some*. Especially in that skeleton costume."

Brooke bustled up, holding her makeup kit.

Emily B. trotted behind.

"Milo, you smudged your blood again!" Brooke scolded. He rolled his eyes, but he let her fix it.

Ms. Ali poked her head in. "Ready, everyone?"

"Ready!" they all yelled.

The skeleton clattered. The zombie howled. The mummy moaned.

Baring his fangs, Milo wished for a moment that he wasn't part of the haunted house. He wanted to come in and get scared.

Of course, he'd never *really* be scared by these tricks.

Crossing his arms, Milo blinked and swallowed.

Nope. Never.

SUPER SLEUTHING STRATEGIES

A few days after Milo and Jazz wrote to Dash Marlowe,
a letter arrived in the mail. . . .

Greetings, Milo and Jazz,
   Congratulations! You did some
super sleuthing in your third case! In
all my detective work, I've never seen a
real ghost. (I thought I did once, in The
Case of the Sheet-Wearing Sneak. But
you can probably guess how that one turned out.)
   To keep your mind *alive* until your next case comes
along, give it a jolt with these mini-mysteries.

Happy Sleuthing!
—*Dash Marlowe*

Warm Up!
These Brain Stretchers are tricky. But remember, the
more you work your brain, the better your brain will
work! You can find the answers at the end of my letter.

1. How do you throw a ball as hard as you can and have
   it come back to you, even if it doesn't hit anything,
   nothing is attached to it, and no one else catches or
   throws it?
2. Two coins make 55 cents and one of them isn't a
   nickel. What are the coins?
3. Can you rearrange the letters in the words "new
   door" to make one word? Note: There is only one
   correct answer.

Spot the Clue!

Strange lights and noises were coming from an old, boarded-up house. Folks in the nearby town said it was haunted. I was curious and decided to investigate.

As soon as I saw the place, I knew there was no ghost. Someone was living there! How did I know? Check out this picture. How many clues can you spot?

Answer: The clues I saw could only mean someone was living in the house: a full bird feeder, laundry on the clothesline, smoke coming from the chimney, a switched-on TV, a cared-for potted plant, and a steaming teakettle. (I soon found out someone was indeed living there—a gentleman with a cat. He said he kept the house looking "haunted" because he hated visitors, and so did his cat. Then he tried to run us out!)

The (Not So) Great Escape: A Logic Puzzle

Three convicts escaped from prison. Can you work out how each one escaped and where they were caught?

Read the clues and fill in the answer box where you can. Then read the clues again to fill in the rest.

1. One prisoner walked out of the prison in disguise.
2. Rocky escaped in the prison garbage truck but didn't get caught at Burger Bob's.
3. The prisoner who dug an escape tunnel got caught at the guard station right outside the prison gate.
4. Louie got caught at Burger Bob's (after a burger).
5. One prisoner got caught robbing the same jewelry store that first landed him in prison.
6. Sal didn't wear a disguise.

Answer Box (see answers on next page)

	Rocky	Louie	Sal
How escaped			
Where caught			

The Shack: A Mini-Mystery

Read this mystery—and try to draw a conclusion!

When I was a boy, my friend Dane and I were off hiking in the woods when it started to rain. We took cover in an old shack. But no sooner did we get inside than the door swung shut and locked. We were trapped!

Dane looked scared. "We'll get out," I told him. "We just need to be logical."

I looked around. There was an open window high up on one wall. But it was too high to reach even when Dane climbed on my shoulders. Then I spotted something. An old shovel propped in the corner. "The floor is dirt," I said. "We can tunnel out!"

We dug and dug. The pile of dirt got bigger and bigger—until we hit solid rock. Tunneling was useless.

But then I noticed something that gave me a new idea. One that was sure to work! So—how did we get out?

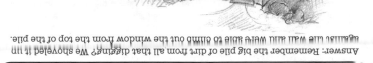

Answer: Remember the big pile of dirt from all that digging? We shoveled it up against the wall and were able to climb out the window from the top of the pile.

Monkey Business: Cause & Effect Mysteries

Think logically about cause and effect! I once investigated a string of animal-related crimes.

CASE NOTEBOOK #17 DM

Take a look at some of my case notes, and see if you can match each motive to the crime!

Motives:

Criminal A wanted to communicate with monkeys.

Criminal B really loved omelets for breakfast.

Criminal C wanted a strange and exotic pet.

Criminal D had a major thirst problem.

Crimes:

A chicken was stolen.

An anteater was smuggled onto a plane.

Someone broke into the zoo's primate section.

A trespasser chased a cow through Farmer Vernon's fields.

Answers: Criminal A was found at the zoo, trying to organize a game of monkey-in-the-middle. Criminal B stole the chicken. He wanted really fresh eggs for his omelet. Criminal C smuggled the anteater onto the plane. He had his strange, exotic pet—until a flight attendant investigated the "strange, exotic smell" coming from his suitcase. Criminal D chased the cow to get a glass of milk. He didn't get one. The cow had been milked that morning.

Answers for Brain Stretchers:

1. Throw the ball straight up in the air.

2. A fifty-cent piece and a nickel. (I said *one* of the coins wasn't a nickel. The other one was!)

3. One word.